Henriette
The Story of a Doll

by TRACY FRIEDMAN

illustrated by VERA ROSENBERRY

SCHOLASTIC INC.

New York Toronto London Auckland Sydney

To my Mom and Dad, and Candy.

Reading level is determined by the
Spache Readability Formula.
3.2 signifies high third grade level.

ISBN 0-590-33842-0

Text copyright © 1986 by Tracy Friedman
Illustrations copyright © 1986 by Vera Rosenberry
All rights reserved. Published by Scholastic Inc.

12 11 10 9 8 7 6 5 4 3 2 1   3   6 7 8 9/8 0 1/9

Printed in the U.S.A.

28

ONE

THE old woman sat wrapped in shawls, staring into the crackling fire. She was holding a letter in her hand and seemed to be deep in thought. She was very old, and all alone in the dusty drawing room, except for a beautiful china doll.

The doll sat on the old woman's lap. She was very elegant. She had bright blue eyes and a lovely painted mouth. Something about the arch of her brow made her seem wise. Her sky blue gown and pink satin slippers were new. But if you looked closely you could see by the thousand tiny cracks in her porcelain face that she, too, was very, very old.

Suddenly the old woman stirred. She tore away a corner of the envelope and a tiny gold locket on a fine gold chain came tumbling out into her hand. She held it up to the firelight to see it more closely. She recognized the locket almost at once. It had belonged to her daughter, who had died somewhere far from home during the war. With trembling fingers she unfolded the letter. The little doll sitting on her lap almost seemed to be reading along.

"She's been found, Henriette. After all these years, my granddaughter has been found."

A smile seemed to flicker across the doll's face. But the old woman shook her head sadly and said, "What's the use? It's too late now. I'm too old, and this broken-down plantation is no place to raise a child. Amanda's better off in the orphanage where some young couple will adopt her. I'll write to the orphanage. I'll explain it to them. They'll understand. . . ."

The old woman got up slowly and walked out of the room. The gold locket, which had been lying in her lap, slipped and slid down the folds of her gown. It fell onto the rug where it lay twinkling in the firelight.

The doll was left sitting alone in the big armchair. The clock ticked. The room was still. Nothing seemed to move. But if you looked closely, you could see tiny crystal tears trickle down the porcelain cheeks and fall silently away.

After a while the doll took a hanky no bigger than a postage stamp out of the pocket of her gown. She blew her nose quietly and dried her tears. She frowned slightly as she always did when she had a difficult decision to make. Then she spoke in a slightly husky voice, with an unmistakable French accent, "I believe in my heart that Amanda is my rightful mistress. If she will not be coming to me, then I should go to her. But how can I leave my old mistress?"

Henriette closed her eyes and remembered the day they had met so many years ago. It was Christmas morning. Henriette had just arrived. She had been sent by steamship all the way to Georgia from the most expensive doll shop in Paris, France. The old woman was a child then.

She had lifted Henriette tenderly from the packing box and whispered, "I shall keep you always, for the rest of my life." That was nearly seventy years ago.

Of course, children do not stay children forever. The little girl had grown up and married. Soon she had a child of her own. Naturally, Henriette had been passed down to that little girl, whose name was Sarah. Henriette had loved her second mistress as she had loved her first. But the years came and went, and one day Sarah kissed Henriette good-bye and ran off to marry a handsome young soldier.

In time Sarah had a daughter, too. The child's name was Amanda, or so the letters said. Henriette was expecting to be packed up and sent off to Amanda, but then the Civil War began. Sarah's letters came less and less often and finally stopped altogether.

When the war was over, the old woman went to the town where Sarah had lived. There was nothing left of it. She found Sarah's grave, but no one knew what had become of Amanda. She began searching for her granddaughter. She made countless trips and wrote hundreds of letters. Finally, she had given up all hope of ever finding the child who had been lost.

"But now she is found! Amanda has been found!" said Henriette to herself. "I belong to her, and she belongs to me. I must go to her." Henriette had made the only decision possible. A doll's place is with the *child* she belongs to.

Now that she knew what she must do, Henriette was eager to be on her way. She climbed up on the arm of the chair and stepped over onto the writing table. Kneeling down on the pad of paper, and using a pen that was very much too large for her, Henriette wrote this note:

> *My dear old friend,*
> *You were my first mistress*
> *and I shall always love you.*
> *But now I must find Amanda, and*
> *if I can I will bring her back to you.*
> *Love H.*

TWO

U NDER ordinary circumstances it should not be difficult for a medium-sized doll, who stands fourteen inches in her stocking feet, to climb down from an armchair. But Henriette was wearing a tight corset and layers of stiff petticoats, which made climbing difficult. By the time she reached the floor, she was exhausted. She sat down on the footstool to catch her breath and consider the journey ahead.

"City Orphanage, Peachtree Street, Atlanta, Georgia." It seemed so far away, but the letter

was quite definite, and the locket was positive proof. It had belonged to Sarah. "Sarah would not have given this locket to anyone but her own daughter," said Henriette. "I must take the locket with me. It belongs to Amanda, just as I do."

Henriette saw the locket lying on the rug a few feet away and went over to it. When she stooped to pick it up, she saw that it had fallen open. Inside were two miniature portraits. One was a handsome young officer in a military uniform; the other was a smiling child with curly black hair. They were pictures of Amanda and her father.

The locket was much too large to wear around her neck, so Henriette tied the chain around her waist and tucked the golden heart into the roomy pocket of her enormous skirt.

On the floor under the curio cabinet was a miniature steamer trunk with leather handles and a shiny brass lock. This trunk was just large enough to contain the extensive wardrobe of a medium-sized doll. Henriette walked over to it, lifted the lid, and pushed back the tray that held dozens of doll-sized bonnets all decorated with feathers, flowers, and frills. She began rummaging in the bottom of the trunk and pulled out a long, red velvet cape.

"This will do nicely," she said to herself as she slipped it on. Of course, the gown she was wearing — sky blue satin with hand-painted pink forget-me-nots — was not ideal for traveling. But Henriette was eager to be on her way. She put a straw bonnet over her honey-colored curls and tied the ribbons under her chin. She squeezed her slender fingers into a tiny pair of white kid gloves and quietly closed the lid. She patted the corner of the trunk fondly, looked back over her shoulder just once, and with a graceful pirouette slipped out the open door.

THREE

THE main hallway of the old plantation house was deserted. Henriette tiptoed along on her soundless satin slippers, crossing under the hall table. She made a wide circle around the grandfather clock, knowing that the tabby cat sometimes took his afternoon nap there.

Most dolls are amazingly skillful at moving about so that no one ever notices, and Henriette was one of the best. As yet she had no complete plan in mind, but experience told her to direct her steps toward that great center of comings and goings, the kitchen.

The kitchen was a big, sunny room with a black-and-white checkerboard floor. The floor usually made Henriette feel like a piece in a chess game. Today she had no thought of games as she darted through the doorway. She ran under a serving table, along the edge of the china cupboard, and slid to a stop behind the great claw foot of the black wood-burning stove.

A little boy was sitting at the kitchen table, dangling his feet, and lazily nibbling a gingersnap. The cook was all the way across the room kneading bread dough. The smell of baking bread was very strong, and it was getting uncomfortably warm under the stove. Still Henriette was patient, listening and waiting for an opportunity to present itself, which presently it did.

The little boy finished the gingersnap and said, "Can I have another cookie?"

"No, sir. You had enough," answered the cook. "Now you get goin' like I said, and hitch that horse up to that wagon."

"How come?"

· "'Cause I told you to."

"But how come?" the boy asked again.

❖◆❖

" 'Cause as soon as the men come up from the fields," the cook explained, "they gonna load that cotton and take it down to the depot."

"How come?"

" 'Cause that cotton's goin' on a train to be sold."

"Where?"

"Atlanta. Now git!"

"Just one more cookie?" said the boy with a grin the cook could not resist.

"All right, just one. And mind you don't leave no crumbs!"

As the little boy settled down to enjoy his last cookie, Henriette began to see a plan taking shape, a plan that revolved around baskets of snowy white cotton just large enough for a medium-sized doll to hide in. It certainly seemed like a possibility.

The cook was humming to herself and thumping away at the bread dough as Henriette crept out of her hiding place and tiptoed across the open floor. She stopped directly under the table, dangerously close to the boy's dangling feet.

Henriette had a remarkable understanding of children, and as a result, could often predict

their behavior. She felt quite certain of what the little boy would do next. Unless she was much mistaken, the two of them would soon be out the door. Henriette held her breath and poised herself for action.

"Come on now, you had enough," the cook said to the boy. "Git goin'."

"Yes, ma'am."

The boy climbed down from his chair and started toward the door. At the last minute, just as Henriette had predicted, he turned back and plunged his fist into the cookie jar. Henriette sprinted like a streak of lightning to the dustpan leaning against the wall. She stooped down and hid behind the dustpan for as long as it took the little boy to snitch one last cookie and run. The boy threw the screen door wide open as he went. Henriette hiked up her skirts and dashed out the door right on the boy's heels.

She was running as fast as she could, but it wasn't fast enough. At the last moment she had to swerve sharply to the left in order to avoid being struck by the slamming door. She lost her balance and found herself sprawling petticoat over pinafore in the shrubbery.

"Mon Dieu!" exclaimed Henriette, in her native language. She often spoke French in moments of stress. "What an undignified position to find oneself in!" But, in fact, Henriette was more surprised than hurt. After she saw that she was safely out of the house she began to feel quite pleased with herself. She brushed the dirt off her gown, straightened her bonnet with a flourish, and flounced off in the direction of a large rhododendron bush.

FOUR

FROM the shade of the large, leafy bush Henriette had a view of the entire yard. The little boy was nowhere to be seen. There was a humming insect sound in the air, and butterflies flirted about in the summertime stillness. Out in the middle of the yard stood the wagon and ten or twelve bushel baskets of cotton, all just waiting, baking in the afternoon sun. Henriette could see waves of heat rising from the dust. She was afraid of bugs and began to wonder if the boll weevils were picked out of the cotton before it was sent off to market. Suddenly Henriette felt light-headed and decided to sit for a moment in the shade.

She leaned back and looked up through the leaves and blossoms to the sky. It seemed so odd to be outside and alone. She was quite used to accompanying her mistresses on trips and outings. As a favorite doll she had traveled widely. But the truth was, she had never been out of doors without a familiar arm around her waist, and so, despite the heat, she began to shiver. Henriette had never considered her size a disadvantage, yet at this moment she felt very small, and Atlanta seemed very far away.

But after a few deep breaths, Henriette's natural courage began to come back. She was a doll with a great deal of determination, even if she was only fourteen inches tall. She knew that if she were separated permanently from her rightful mistress the result would be a broken heart, perhaps two. So she lifted up her tiny chin, threw her cape back over her shoulder, and marched directly toward the nearest basket of cotton.

Up close the baskets were much larger than

they had looked from across the yard. Her idea was to climb into one of them. But how. . . ? Henriette walked around the group of baskets twice, but she did not see anything that could be used as a stepping stone. She did, however, notice a sturdy rake leaning up against the wagon. It was rusty and caked with mud, yet the solid iron teeth looked, from Henriette's point of view, quite a bit like the rungs of a ladder.

Knocking the rake over was simple enough. The tall handle made it top heavy. Henriette gave it just the tiniest shove and gravity took over. The hard part was standing the rake up on its side. Henriette wrestled with the rake for quite some time before she managed to lift it into place. After testing it to see that her make-shift ladder was secure, she noticed that she had ruined her lovely white kid gloves. "Oh, well. *C'est la vie,*" she whispered to herself with only a tiny trace of sadness.

Henriette climbed the rake carefully, hand over hand, with her skirts stuffed under her arm. When she reached the top she saw a sight that took her breath away. Spread out before her, as if she had climbed a ladder to heaven, was a vast cluster of white cotton clouds — great cumulous puffs. Henriette was standing there admiring the view, when suddenly a yellow mutt with big, floppy ears came trotting around the corner of the barn.

The dog came zigzagging across the yard at a speed that showed more energy than common sense. From experience Henriette knew this could mean trouble. She stepped onto the edge of the basket and threw herself forward into the cotton, knocking the rake over as she fell. All this activity caught the pup's eye, and he headed toward her with reckless curiosity.

The pup had no idea what to make of this tiny lady in satin and lace. He began questioning her with a steady stream of snuffles, yaps, growls, and barks, jumping and dancing as if he couldn't stand still. Henriette was afraid that the noise would bring the cook out of the kitchen. She knelt at the edge of the basket and whispered to the pup in French. "Hush, hush, *mon petit chien.*" Henriette always found

that the sound of her native language had a soothing effect on animals.

The pup did seem to respond. He stopped barking, put his chin down on his front paws, and cocked his head slightly to the side. This was merely the quiet before the storm. The next moment Henriette found herself nose to nose with the pup. He was standing on his hind legs, yapping and barking, and rocking the basket wildly with each wag of his tail.

Henriette was not cruel by nature, but it was clear that something had to be done. She took aim and slapped the pup as hard as she could on the nose. The pup let out a yelp. He was not hurt, but his feelings were. He walked away and flopped down in the dust, looking miserable. Henriette decided it was time to put some distance between herself and the dog.

It was the oddest sensation, walking and sinking in billows of cotton. She climbed over the side of one basket and tumbled into the next. When she was safely surrounded by a basket or two on each side, she began to burrow into the cotton. Soon the little bed she was making for herself was just the right size. She felt in her pocket to make sure the locket was still there, then snuggled down and covered herself with a white cotton cloud. She felt safe and comfy and just barely remembered hearing the men's voices mixed with the barking of the dog as she drifted off to sleep.

FIVE

ENRIETTE was dreaming that she was on a train. She could almost feel the motion and hear the wheels clacking along the track. Little by little the lurching and swaying became more real. The dream began to seem less like a dream. Suddenly Henriette was wide awake. She sat up with a start, sending cotton balls flying hither and thither.

One glance told her that she was in a huge boxcar. She couldn't believe her eyes. Just moments ago she had dozed off in her own backyard. Now she was on a train speeding toward Atlanta.

In addition to the baskets of cotton, Henriette was surrounded by sacks of grain, boxes of vegetables, and even a crate with several noisy chickens clucking away inside. The far end of the car was loaded with luggage. Trunks and suitcases were piled nearly to the ceiling. There were doors at each end of the car, but no windows.

Although it was tempting to stay right where she was, Henriette knew it was time to leave her cozy bed.

She climbed out of the basket onto a nearby crate. Then, like a miniature mountain climber, she made her way over piles of feed sacks, through valleys of vegetable boxes, and finally down along the aisle that ran through the center of the car. She tiptoed past the crate of hens and ducked under a jagged ledge or two. She prayed that no sudden lurch of the train would start an avalanche.

When she reached the far end of the car she began looking for something. An idea? A possibility? Even Henriette could not have told you exactly what she was looking for.

Presently she spotted a hatbox sitting high on top of a stack of suitcases. Henriette remembered one just like it as a favorite hiding place and wanted to take a closer look. The convenient placement of several suitcases of assorted sizes and shapes formed a kind of staircase. Henriette lifted her skirts and practically skipped up toward the hatbox.

It was indeed very much like the one she had known. A leather strap at just the right height fastened the lid. "I could hide in this hatbox," she thought as she unbuckled the strap. "But then who knows where I might end up."

She meant to lift the lid just an inch or so to peek inside. Instead she received the fright of her life. Henriette let out a scream, and the lid went flying. She staggered backward and fell flat on her back with her tiny heart pounding.

Staring down at her from the top of the strangest hat she had ever seen was a huge stuffed pigeon. It had beady glass eyes. Its wings were spread, and its beak was open,

ready to gobble up the next worm that came along.

"*Mon Dieu!* What a hideous hat!" exclaimed Henriette, as she straightened her own simple straw bonnet. "Well, that certainly concludes that! I would not consider sharing a hatbox with such a beast!"

Henriette spent the next few minutes hauling the lid back into place. When she was finished, she realized there was nothing to do now but wait. She sat down and arranged her skirts in a ladylike fashion. She was humming *"Freres Jacques"* and picking cotton fuzz off her red velvet cape when the door at the far end of the car slammed open. Two children came racing down the aisle heading directly toward her.

SIX

As luck would have it, the children were playing a game of tag and didn't notice Henriette. When the boy reached the door just inches from where she sat, he found it was locked. The girl had him cornered. She tagged him on the shoulder and ran back in the direction from which they had come, yelling, "You're it. I tagged you. You're it!"

"That's not fair. The door was locked," hollered her brother, but he ran after her anyway.

Halfway down the aisle the little girl tripped

and went sprawling. Her brother tagged her before she could get up.

"You're it again. Ha, ha, Louise. You're always it!"

"I am not!"

"Yes, you are. You're always it!"

"Well, I don't want to play anymore. So there!" said Louise. She turned on her heel and wandered off among the boxes and trunks.

During all of this Henriette had simply frozen. She didn't breathe, or move a muscle. She was praying they wouldn't notice her. Ordinarily Henriette loved children, but these two looked like trouble. Suddenly Louise spotted her.

"Hey, Homer. Look. There's a doll sitting here."

"Who cares? It's just an old doll. Let's play tag."

"You go play tag. I'm going to play with this doll," said Louise as she grabbed Henriette roughly by the waist. She turned Henriette this way and that, pulling her curls, and pinching her arms. She yanked up Henriette's skirt, counted her petticoats, and turned her upside down to look at the lace on her pantaloons. It

didn't take long for Louise to notice the locket. It had fallen out of Henriette's pocket and was dangling from the chain around her waist.

In an instant Louise had the locket in her possession. She looked it over, front and back, and jammed her fingernail between the two halves to open it. She didn't notice the severe scowl on Henriette's face.

"Hey look, pictures," said Louise.

"Let me see," said Homer, snatching the locket away.

"Give me back my locket!" said Louise with a howl.

"If I give it back what will you give me?"

"A penny."

"All right. Fair trade."

Homer was trying to decide what to spend the penny on while Louise wrapped the dainty chain around her wrist. When she got it fastened, Louise held her arm up in the air like a model in a mail-order catalogue and admired the shiny gold trinket. Homer decided he'd probably buy a cat's-eye marble with his penny.

But in the meantime, he still felt like playing tag.

"Come on, Louise. Let's play tag. You're it!" He yanked one of his sister's pigtails and dashed off in the direction of the open door.

Louise yelped in pain and yelled, "I'll get you for that, Homer!" She ran off after her brother, taking Henriette with her.

SEVEN

HOMER ran as fast as he could. Hair-pulling was something Louise didn't take lightly. Henriette was carried along on a breakneck dash through the train. They ran from car to car, slamming doors open and shut, and bumping passengers along the way.

Louise didn't catch up with Homer until he reached the compartment where their mother sat reading. Homer thought that his mother's presence would keep Louise from taking revenge. But he was wrong. Henriette found herself in the middle of a fist fight, during which she received several blows and lost a shoe.

"Stop it, children. Homer! Louise! What's this all about?"

"Homer pulled my hair!"

"I did not."

"Yes, you did!"

"Louise found this doll, and she won't let me play with her," said Homer. He snatched Henriette away from Louise.

"She's my doll. I found her!" hollered Louise, grabbing for Henriette.

"I'll settle it," said the children's mother as she shoved Henriette into the corner of the overhead luggage rack. "Neither of you will play with her. Now I want both of you to sit down, and I don't want to see either of you move a muscle. Is that understood?"

"Yes, ma'am." The children slumped down into their seats. Their mother gave them one last glare and went back to her book.

In all her life Henriette had never received such treatment. Like any doll she loved a good game, but this was too much. Henriette seldom became angry, but she was angry now! She wanted to stamp her foot and tell those rough-necks a thing or two. She felt tears welling up in her eyes, but she wasn't about to let them see her cry so she choked back her anger.

She knew that Homer and Louise weren't trying to be mean, but that didn't help. Her whole body was sore and stiff from being manhandled. Her gown had been torn, her pride was injured, and one of her lovely pink satin slippers was lost. But worse than that, Amanda's locket had been stolen. Henriette knew she must get it back. But how? She glanced down at the two children. Louise was playing a game of tic-tac-toe. Homer was busy pulling the buttons off the upholstery.

"I must be patient," Henriette thought. "There is a long train ride ahead. I shall think of something."

Henriette was grateful that the children's mother had put her out of harm's way, but she was also very uncomfortable wedged into the corner of the luggage rack. Very carefully, in the way dolls have that no one ever notices, Henriette shifted her position. She straightened her bonnet, smoothed her hair, and folded her hands on her lap. Just about then the conductor came down the aisle outside the compartment announcing, "Atlanta, Georgia. Next station stop Atlanta, Georgia."

Henriette was amazed. Atlanta had seemed so far away. How could they have arrived so quickly?

"All right, children. We're almost there. Louise, put your hat on. Homer, take my dressing case. Come now, children, follow me."

The train had pulled into the station. The family was leaving the compartment. They had forgotten all about Henriette. What should she do? She couldn't let Louise walk out the door wearing Amanda's locket. Without hesitation Henriette leaned forward and called Louise by name.

Now, you understand, dolls speak to children in a most unusual way. It's not something that we're ever really aware of. Their voices have a melody and pitch that you can't hear at all after a certain age. Even when you're young, you don't hear them in the same way you hear other voices. Yet dolls do speak to children every day, all over the world, just as Henriette was speaking to Louise. All she had to do was call her name.

"Oh, Mama," said Louise, "I almost forgot that doll. Can I take her with me?"

"Well, I suppose it's all right. She doesn't seem to belong to anyone." The children's mother got Henriette down from the luggage rack and handed her to Louise. "Come along now, and don't dawdle."

So Henriette, Louise, Homer, and the children's mother all left the train together. They marched through the crowded station in military fashion, and Louise hung on tightly to Henriette all the way.

EIGHT

THE street outside the station was jammed with coaches and carriages. People on foot and on horseback were coming and going in a great hurry. Henriette, who was used to the quiet of the country, found all the noise and bustle a little frightening.

The children's mother led them straight up to a carriage for hire. She put the children inside the carriage and began giving the porter instructions about the luggage. The large trunks were lifted to the roof, the smaller bags were stowed inside, the door was slammed, and they were off.

Homer and Louise were glued to the windows as they drove through the streets of Atlanta. Henriette was sitting in the crook of Louise's arm and had a perfect view of the city as it went by. The children were counting brass-topped hitching posts. It was a game — the first one to spot twenty was the winner. Ordinarily Henriette would have joined in, secretly and silently pitting herself against the other players. Today she had more important business on her mind. She was watching the street signs: Main Street, Central Street, Washington, Grove Street, Elm Street, Magnolia . . . Peachtree!

In answer to a prayer he couldn't possibly have heard, the driver turned when they reached the corner. As they drove along Peachtree, Henriette looked carefully at every building. She saw the Public Library, the Post Office, and City Hall. They passed a hospital, several banks, a church, and finally there it was — a large gray building with the words carved in stone above the door . . . City Orphanage.

Several children were playing jump rope out

on the stoop. One little girl had curly black hair, but it wasn't Amanda. At least it didn't look like the picture in the locket. Of course, children do change, and perhaps the picture wasn't a good likeness. Still, Henriette had a feeling deep down inside that she would know Amanda the moment she saw her. You see, there's a strong bond between a doll and the child she belongs to. Call it nonsense, or a sixth sense, but it's something that most dolls believe in.

The carriage drove on. A tiny sigh was heard as the orphanage disappeared from view. Right about then Homer spotted the twentieth hitching post. He began bouncing up and down on the seat, chanting, "I won, I won, I won."

"Homer always wins," said Louise.

"Never mind, dear," said the children's mother. "Why don't you play with your doll?"

Louise began poking halfheartedly at Henriette's clothing. She took off the little straw bonnet and the cape and tossed them on the seat. She twirled Henriette around once or twice, and then put her aside. Louise just sat there staring out the window. Her mother asked her what was wrong. Louise answered with an enormous yawn. They had been traveling since dawn, and she was sleepy.

Louise curled up on the seat and quickly dropped off to sleep. Henriette had been waiting for a chance to recover the locket and now it had come. Louise's arm, with the dainty chain wrapped around the wrist, had nearly fallen into Henriette's lap. Homer was looking out the

window, shooting pedestrians with an imaginary pistol. The children's mother was trying to finish the book she had been reading. No one was watching. Quickly and quietly Henriette went to work. Her tiny fingers were just the right size for the delicate clasp. In the twinkling of an eye, the precious golden locket was returned safe and sound to Henriette's pocket.

When the carriage came to a stop Homer jumped out. He ran into the house shouting, "We're home, Dad. We're home." After a moment the children's father came outside. He greeted his wife, then picked up sleeping Louise and carried her into the house. The children's mother took her book and dressing case, and followed along.

Henriette was alone in the carriage. She knew what she must do. She jumped to her feet, scooped up her hat and cape, and threw them to the floor. She sat down on the edge of the seat, rolled over on her tummy, then lowered herself by her hands. She hung suspended in the air for a moment, then dropped to the floor.

As she fell her enormous skirt billowed up around her like a parachute.

The butler came out the door and headed down the stairs toward the carriage. Henriette grabbed her belongings and ducked under the seat. The butler unloaded the luggage, tipped the driver, and went back into the house. The carriage was miles away before anyone in the family noticed that Henriette was gone.

NINE

HENRIETTE was a secret passenger in the carriage for several days. The coachman never knew he had a stowaway aboard. She planned to stay hidden under the seat until a passenger asked for an address on Peachtree. When the carriage stopped to drop off the paying customer, Henriette would hop out and go her merry way.

While Henriette was traveling the streets of Atlanta, the old woman was fretting over the loss of her doll. After finishing the letter to the orphanage, and posting it, she had returned to the drawing room. Henriette was nowhere to be found. The old woman looked everywhere. She didn't find Henriette, but she did find a note with tiny, perfectly elegant writing.

At first the old woman didn't believe that the note was from Henriette. She thought that someone was playing a trick on her. For several days she suspected the cook's son and was quite cross with him. But as the days went by it became clear that Henriette was really gone. The old woman sat in her armchair, reading the note over and over again.

Henriette traveled the streets of Atlanta for three days, listening carefully to each address as the driver picked up and dropped off passengers. The hours seemed very long, but Henriette didn't mind. She found a treasure of lost objects under the seat that helped to pass the time. There was an old newspaper, which she read from front to back, a handful of coins for spinning and stacking, a set of keys, two penny postcards, and a slingshot. Henriette wondered if the slingshot belonged to Homer. She also found an embroidered handbag and made herself quite comfortable using it as a cushion.

About the middle of the third afternoon a gentleman got into the carriage and asked to be taken to Twenty-nine Peachtree. This was what Henriette had been waiting for. She put on her hat and cape, and was ready to go when the carriage stopped. The man got out at the curb and shut the door. Henriette tiptoed to the other door. She reached up, grabbed the handle, and pulled down with all her might. The carriage door sprung open.

Just as Henriette stepped out onto the running board, a fire wagon went charging by with the bell clanging. It was followed by another wagon and two men on horseback going just as fast. On the other side of the road, buggies and riders were speeding by in a steady stream. Henriette could see that a busy city street was no place for a medium-sized china doll.

She was about to jump back inside when the driver cracked the whip. The carriage took off and went bouncing down the street. The first jolt knocked Henriette off her feet. The second almost knocked her off the running board. She

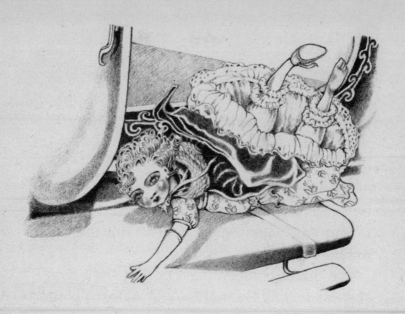

was hanging on for dear life and praying as the ground rushed by beneath her feet. The unlatched door slammed and banged above her head.

Suddenly the carriage stopped. The driver had realized that the door was open and came around to close it. He found a very frightened china doll, half on and half off the running board.

"Now, what's a little slip of a thing like you doing out here?" said the driver as he picked up Henriette with his big strong hands and wiped a spot of dirt off her nose.

"Some little girl must have left you behind. Funny, I don't remember carrying any children today. It must have been that little girl a couple of days ago. Sure, I remember — a little girl with braids, and a brother. Seems to me I dropped them off over on Maple Street. She'll be missing you, that's for sure. Well, I can't be taking you back today. Haven't got the time. Maybe tomorrow."

The driver climbed back up into the driver's seat. He tucked Henriette snugly into the corner on a folded-up blanket. "Now, you just stay put, Missy. You'll be better off up here with me than out on that running board!"

He cracked the whip, and once more they were under way. Henriette's little heart was still pounding furiously. She had been frightened, but she felt safe now with this kind man by her side.

Henriette rode around in the driver's seat all day. She felt like a little princess out on a sightseeing tour. When the City Hall clock struck nine, the coachman headed for home. He pulled the carriage into the yard and put the horse in the stable.

"Now, it's in out of the rain for you, little Miss Muffet!" he said as he lifted Henriette down from the driver's seat and put her inside the carriage. "Sleep tight tonight. In the morning I'll be taking you home." He closed the door and went off to his supper.

Henriette was once again left alone with a decision to make. It didn't matter how nice the coachman was. She couldn't stay here and allow herself to be returned to Louise. She had to find Amanda! It was clear that the city streets were too dangerous during daylight hours. She would have to set off on foot at night, while the city slept.

TEN

HENRIETTE waited until midnight, then opened the carriage door and peered out into the dark. The stable yard was deserted. All the lights were out in the house. No one was stirring. She climbed out of the carriage and dropped lightly to the ground. The yard was filled with junk, and there were big muddy puddles in the ruts made by the carriage wheels. The ground felt cold through the stocking on her shoeless foot. Henriette picked her way carefully across the yard and headed down the alley that led to the street.

When she got to the corner she looked to the left and to the right. She had no idea which way to go. Off in the distance she saw a clock in a tower and decided she might as well head in that direction.

She walked along at a steady pace, passing in and out of the shadows cast by the street-lamps. The clock in the tower kept striking the hours away. She wasn't hurrying and she wasn't afraid. It was a lovely night, with a warm breeze and a bright moon, and she had the city all to herself.

She walked and walked, down block after endless block, past rows of houses that all looked alike. At every corner she stopped to read the street signs. She still had not found the orphanage when the clock struck one.

On and on she walked, past a vacant lot, a school yard, and a cemetery. Suddenly a news-paper blew across her path, and a bird swooped down at her out of the dark. She hurried on a little faster as the clock struck two.

As Henriette walked along, the houses got bigger and more elegant. Many had huge lawns with black iron fences and brass-topped hitching posts. She stopped to rub a sore spot on her foot as the clock struck three.

The night was slipping away. Henriette was loosing heart. There was no sign of the orphanage. What if she was going in the wrong direction? She was walking as fast as she could, but it was a huge city, and she was only a medium-sized doll.

Finally the street led to a park. Henriette heard splashing water and saw a graceful little fountain bubbling away in the moonlight. She limped over and sat down on the edge of the pool. She heaved a great sigh for a small doll

and reached into her pocket. She sat for quite some time gazing sadly at Amanda's portrait. Henriette was feeling lonely and wondered if Amanda was lonely, too. She thought about the old woman sitting alone in her armchair and wondered if leaving had been a mistake. The wind ruffled the trees overhead. Thin fingers of clouds chased across the sky as the clock struck four.

Henriette realized how far she had come when she saw that the clock tower was just across the street . . . in the City Hall . . . right next to the Post Office! Suddenly Henriette knew where she was! The carriage had passed this way on the first day, right after leaving the train station. The orphanage was just up ahead, on the other side of the park.

Henriette wasn't tired any longer. She began running as fast as she could. She ran past park benches and flower beds, her little red cape streaming out behind her. She felt light as air and very happy. She ran and ran, across the street, and up the block. She didn't stop until she reached the orphanage.

ELEVEN

THE gray stone building looked very forbid-
ding with all the windows dark. The huge
oak door was closed and locked for the night.
Henriette ran up and beat her tiny fists against
the door. It wouldn't budge. She paced back
and forth, trying to decide what to do. Finally
she sat down on the stoop, folded her arms
across her chest, and said loudly enough for
anyone within earshot to hear, "I shall simply
sit here until morning, if need be. Then I will

ask the first person who comes along to ring the bell for me."

As it happened, the only one within earshot was a black and orange calico cat. She had been watching Henriette with great curiosity from the top of the porch railing and wanted to take a closer look. She dropped gracefully to the ground and circled Henriette cautiously.

Henriette was not in the mood to be bothered. She told the cat to go away. But the cat was not used to taking orders. She prowled around at a leisurely pace, then sat down a few feet away and stared at Henriette. Henriette stared right back. It was a contest that Henriette lost in the end. Something about the cat's expression made Henriette very uncomfortable. She turned her back and pretended to ignore the cat. But she could feel those enormous eyes staring at her, and the cat's purring sounded like thunder. When she couldn't stand it any longer, Henriette got up and marched off, along the front of the building. The cat slinked along behind, her eyes glowing amber in the dark.

Henriette never really knew whether she followed the cat or if the cat followed her. But together, they made their way under a fence, over a drainpipe, and through some bushes to the back of the building.

The rear entrance to the orphanage was at the foot of a short flight of stairs. The cat paused, looked knowingly at Henriette out of the corner of her eye, then glided down the stairs and disappeared. It was too dark for Henriette to see where the cat had gone, yet she knew she must follow.

At the bottom of the stairs, right next to the large door, was a miniature swinging door. It was a private entrance, so the calico cat could come and go at will. Henriette barely managed to squeeze through on her hands and knees. Her hoopskirt kept getting in the way. When she was safely inside she looked around for her calico friend. The cat was sitting high on top of the china cabinet, licking one of her dainty white paws. Henriette tried to get her attention to say thank you, but the cat just looked at her as if she were yesterday's leftovers, and went back to licking her paw. Henriette smiled to herself and tiptoed out of the kitchen.

TWELVE

A dark passageway led to the front hall. Henriette moved along cautiously. She guessed that the children's bedrooms were on the second floor, and so she was looking for the staircase. When she found it, she was staggered by its size. The stairs rose upward on a steep curve to an enormous height. Henriette took a deep breath and began climbing.

One step at a time, Henriette struggled upwards, climbing higher and higher. When she finally reached the top, she turned and looked back down from where she had come. It was like looking down the side of a mountain. Henriette prayed with all her heart and soul that Amanda's bedroom wasn't on the third floor.

Leaving the staircase behind, Henriette tiptoed down the empty hallway. She paused at several open doors, but each time moved quietly on. When she reached the last room at the end of the hall, she stepped through the doorway without hesitation. She found herself in a large dormitory. There were twenty beds, with twenty little girls sleeping peacefully, but Henriette only had eyes for one.

In the last bed on the left lay a little girl with curly black hair. Moonlight coming through the window fell gently across her face. Henriette walked straight down the aisle between the rows of beds. The rest of the world ceased to exist as she was drawn toward that circle of light and the child sleeping at its center.

Henriette climbed up on the chair next to the bed. Without looking twice she knew that she had found Amanda. The curving cheek and long dark lashes were exactly like those in the miniature portrait. She was the very image of her mother, and her grandmother before her.

But more importantly, Henriette felt a strange tingling sensation. It had started under her heart, and had grown and grown, until she could feel it from the tips of her fingers to the soles of her feet. Every beat of her heart seemed to be saying, "I belong to you, and you belong to me." She couldn't take her eyes off Amanda. She couldn't believe she had finally come home. You see, for dolls as well as people, home is where the heart is.

From the chair it was easy to step over onto the bed. Henriette walked softly across the folds in the bedclothes and hung her hat and cape neatly on the headboard. She took the locket out of her pocket and polished it on the hem of her skirt. She knelt down and fastened the dainty chain around Amanda's neck. Being very careful not to wake her, Henriette whispered, "I made a promise to my oldest friend that I will try to keep. But that journey will have to wait. For now it is enough that we are together." Then she lay down, put her head on Amanda's shoulder, and went to sleep.

Several weeks later the director of the orphanage wrote a letter to the old woman relating some strange information concerning her granddaughter, the locket, and a china doll. The old woman, sitting in her armchair in front of the crackling fire, smiled to herself as she read the letter. She was not surprised at all. In her heart she had always known where Henriette had gone.

No one at the orphanage was ever able to figure out how Amanda's shiny gold locket had been returned to her, or where the beautiful French doll with the torn and muddy dress had come from. But it was clear for all to see that Henriette and Amanda belonged together, and no one ever thought to part them.